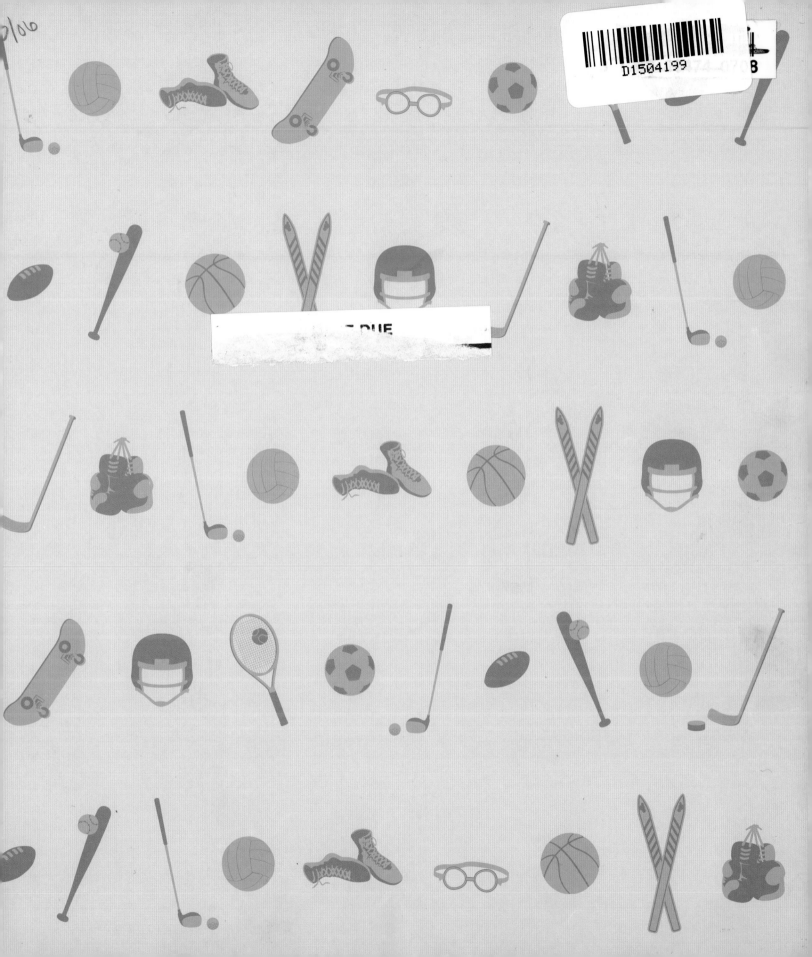

This book belongs to:

_____

Age:

_____

Date:

_____

Favorite Sport:

Alexander, It's Time For Bed!

Written by Alex Lluch

Illustrated by David Defenbaugh

Wedding Solutions Publishing, Inc.
San Diego, California

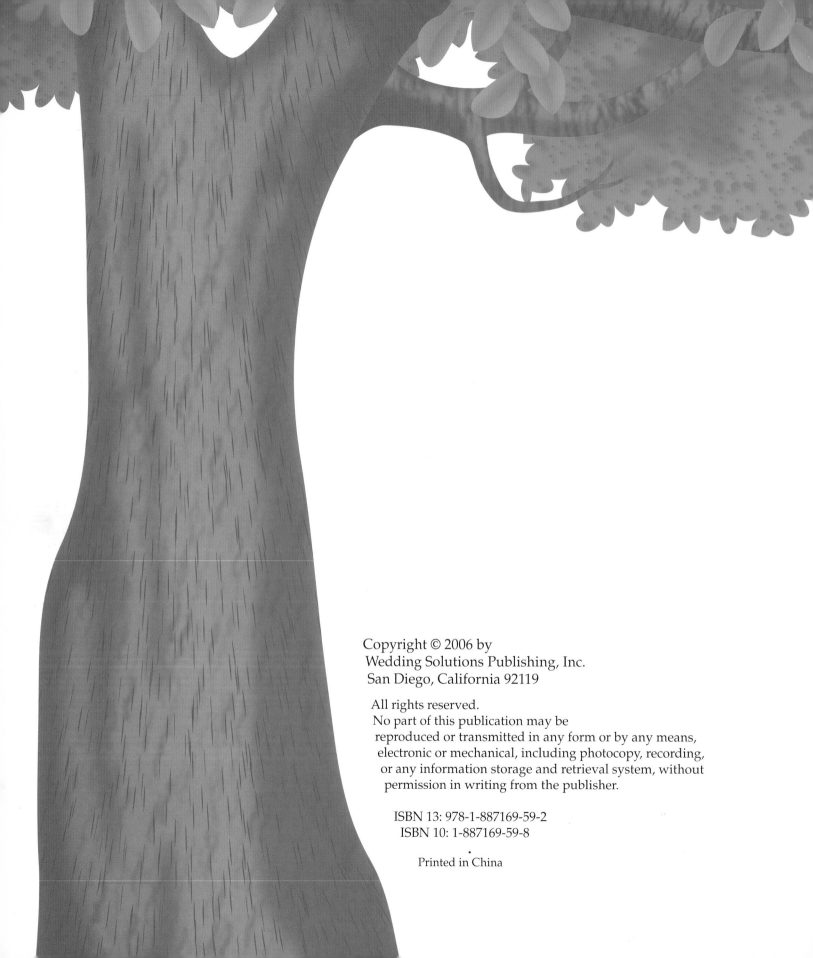

ISBN 13: 978-1-887169-59-2
ISBN 10: 1-887169-59-8

.
Printed in China

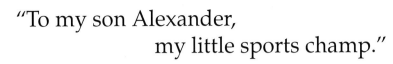

"To my son Alexander,
    my little sports champ."

– Alex Lluch

What did I hear? What did she say?
I don't want to sleep. I just want to play!

Sleeping is the last thing in my head.
There is no way I can go to bed!

But a game of soccer could make me tired!
Then I wouldn't be so worked-up and wired!

Or I could go running. I sprint like a cat.
I can run a whole mile in five seconds flat.

What about volleyball? That's what I like!
No one can stop my powerful spike.

But math and numbers, they're not my thing.
I'd rather throw punches and box in the ring.

When I wrestle, my opponents fear the ground.
I can take them down in just the first round!

I can also use karate to kick and to fight.
I am a champion, a mightiful might!

Hey, a swimming race is what I must do.
That would wash my face and my whole body too!

Or I could go surfing, that would be slick.
The cold ocean water would sure do the trick!

And if it gets too cold, I'll head for the bay.
I'll water ski happily all through the day.

Brush my teeth? That's no fun!
I'd rather go skiing in the bright winter sun.

I also like snowboarding. Now that's a great thrill.
Everyone calls me the "King of the Hill."

Hockey is a game for those who are rough.
If you want to survive, you have to be tough.

My favorite book is all about sports.
But when I play football, I get out of sorts.

I do like baseball, that's really for me.
I can hit home runs as far as you see.

I'm great at basketball, even though I'm small.
I can slam dunk like I'm ten feet tall.

I wouldn't disobey, I wouldn't dare.
But I'd rather skateboard and do flips in the air.

I look forward to winter, I love my ice skates.
I can dance to the music and do figure eights.

I like to dive off boards that are narrow.
And enter the water as straight as an arrow.

Oh, please, pretty please, with a cherry on top.
A quick game of golf, and then I will stop.

Or what about tennis? Now that's a fun sport.
You have to be quick to rule on the court.

I also like gymnastics, I like all the sports.
Instead of pajamas, I'd rather wear shorts.

Alexan
go to be

There's no time for bed, there's no time to rest.
You must practice, practice, practice, if you want to be the best.

But never forget the old golden rule,
or you'll get in trouble at home and at school.

It says: "Listen to your parents, teachers and coaches.
Or you'll end up living in a place full of roaches!"

And believe in yourself, that's what you must do,
if you want to be a champion, and successful too.

Tomorrow will be another great day.
I can't wait to wake up and go out to play.

Kids' Fitness

There is no question that sports are good for growing children. Activities that provide exercise and social interaction are essential for child development. But with all the options, from football to gymnastics, how do you know which sport would be most beneficial for your children? The key is to introduce children to several different types of activities and determine what they enjoy and are good at. Encourage your children to participate in activities that are fun, keep them moving, and that they like. Sports will not only promote good health, but your children will also be learning to share, make friends, and develop their self-esteem.

What Parents Can Do

Keep your children motivated by focusing on their talents and achievements. If your children love being in the water, suggest that they take up swimming. Always be sure to provide plenty of positive reinforcement and occasions where your children can nurture their talents. Support and encourage your children by attending as many games and meets as you can. Another great way to be involved is through organized family activities. Taking your children on a family bike ride or swimming at your local pool is a wonderful way for everyone to spend time together and get some exercise!

Bedtime Tips

Bedtime doesn't have to be a chore! Create a routine that makes "going to bed" a special time. Develop a ritual that your child can look forward to each night.

Incorporate a favorite bedtime story or song, or ask your child about his or her day. Something as simple as a hug, kiss, and telling your child "I love you" each night can make bedtime a positive experience. By establishing a reliable routine, you are creating good bedtime habits that both you and your child can enjoy.

Getting your children to bed can be easier if their bedroom is a place that they love and feel secure spending time in. Let your children participate in decorating the room. Allow them to help you select blankets and pillows to make the bed a cozy place where they are comfortable. The more the room reflects your children's taste, the more willingly they will sleep in it!

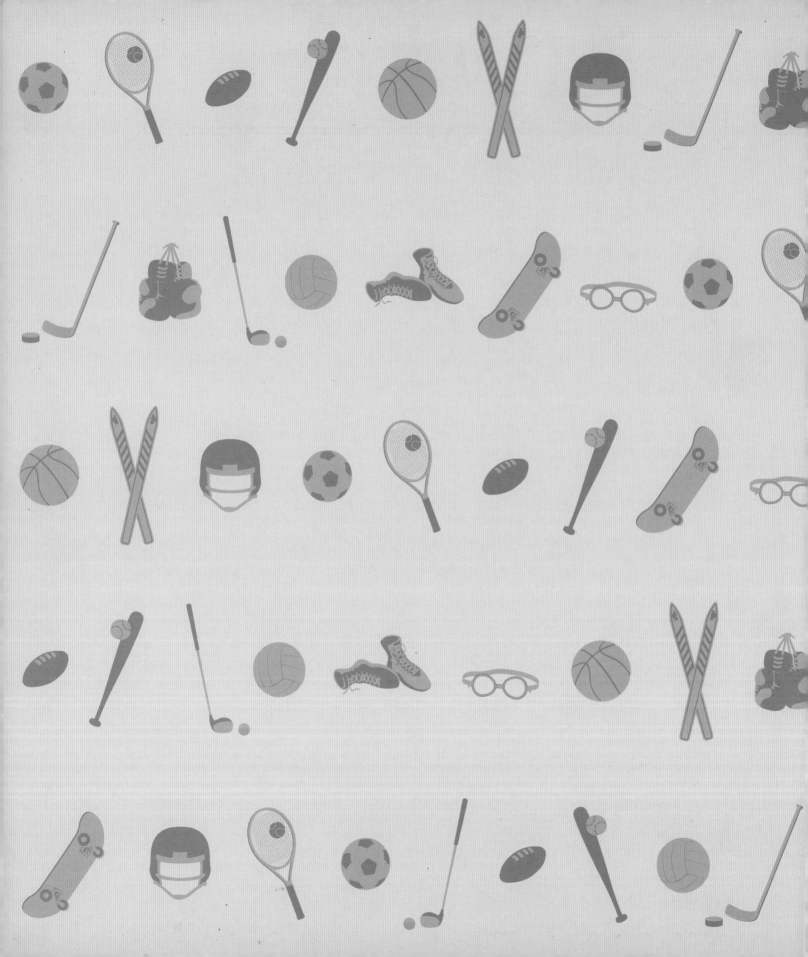